This edition published by Parragon Books Ltd in 2013

Parragon Books Ltd
Chartist House
15–17 Trim Street
Bath BA1 1HA, UK
www.parragon.com

ISBN 978-1-4723-3211-0

Printed in China

ROBO KNIGHT

Bath • New York • Singapore • Hong Kong • Cologne • Delhi
Melbourne • Amsterdam • Johannesburg • Shenzhen

On the edge of a forest outside of the city, a group of students gathered in front of Mr Burley.

"Okay class. Everyone find a study buddy to partner up with. Remember to keep your eyes peeled for anything important." As he finished speaking, Mr Burley stood on the end of a discarded rake, which flipped up and hit him in the face!

"You okay, Mr B?" asked Jake Hollings, trying hard not to laugh.

"Yup," replied Mr Burley, as he crumpled to the ground.

Sometime later, Emma Goodall and Noah Carver were walking through a dark part of the forest when Emma noticed something odd.

"Noah! Look!" she called, pointing to a stream trickling out from behind an abandoned building.

"It's just the old factory," frowned Noah. "It closed down years ago because of too much pollution."

"You're right," agreed Emma, "but just look at the colour of that water. Looks like the chemicals are still seeping through."

"They probably have been for all these years," agreed Noah, reaching over to collect some toxic goo in a vial. "I'll analyze this back –"

But before he could finish his sentence, he was interrupted by a blood-curdling scream.

Noah and Emma glanced at one another for a split second, before racing in the direction of the trouble.

Emma and Noah pushed through a crowd of their fellow students to see what was going on. Mr Burley was standing with their friends Troy Burrows, Jake Hollings and Gia Morgan. They were inspecting an ENORMOUS footprint!

"Great Caesar's salad!" gasped Mr Burley. "Bigfoot was here! Uh ... the fieldtrip is over. We'd better get back to the bus."

As the students hurried off, Troy and Jake exchanged knowing looks.

"Bigfoot?" queried Troy doubtfully.

"No," said Jake, shaking his head. "There is no such thing. This must be some kind of hoax."

Back at school, Jake and Gia were at their lockers when their Morphers beeped and summoned them to the plaza. The pair hurried there without delay and were quickly joined by Troy, Emma and Noah. The five teenagers were preparing for action when they heard a loud HISS behind them!

The team spun round and was confronted by a terrible snake-headed monster. Immediately, they each pulled out their Morpher and they transformed into the Megaforce Rangers.

As the Rangers prepared for battle, two more mutant monsters, Bluefur and Bigs, materialized out of nowhere!

"It's time to destroy some humans," said Bluefur, towering above them. "My toxic venom will annihilate all of you."

"That's not going to happen," cried Blue Ranger.

Bluefur was furry, spiky and horribly rude. In his razor-like claws he carried a ferocious-looking, double-headed club. Bigs was huge and blobby, with terrifying tentacles.

"I'll stomp you all into dust," snarled Bluefur, stamping his huge foot on the ground, leaving behind a familiar footprint.

"Bigfoot," gasped Pink Ranger. "But how?"

"We rose from the toxic sludge you humans left behind when you closed down that factory," Bluefur said. "Now we've joined forces with the bugs and Vrak to take you humans out."

"You brought this upon yourselves," added Bigs. "Think of how harmful toxins are to you and then imagine how it'd feel to be MADE of them!"

As the mutant monsters prepared to attack, the Rangers leaped into action. Red Ranger thrust his sword at Bigs but it bounced off his jelly-like belly.

"Once you attack you'll become part of a sludge pile," gloated Bigs, knocking Red Ranger to the ground.

Pink Ranger leapt to Red Ranger's side, determined to help defend her friend.

The other Rangers charged in to help, too. They flipped, kicked, blasted and slashed, but it was no good. One by one, the Rangers were brought to their knees by the terrifying mutants.

"These humans are even weaker than I expected," laughed Bluefur evilly.

"No. We're just much stronger." Bigs cackled so hard that his enormous belly wobbled like a repulsive jelly. "More pollution every day means more and more power for us! Mighty mutants!"

The Rangers rose as one to confront their evil foes again. But before they could do anything, Hisser erupted from the ground, spraying out great globules of green slime.

The teenagers gasped and tried to escape but it was no good. The green slime turned brown and it quickly began to sap their strength.

Bigs and Bluefur laughed as they watched the Rangers fall to the ground.

"Once you're all gone, we're going to break open chemical tanks everywhere," gloated Bigs.

"The Earth will become a sea of slime," added Hisser gleefully. "A paradise for mutants and a graveyard for humans."

The Rangers summoned every last ounce of strength they had and charged, but Hisser quickly overcame them with his deadly slime. The vile villain was just about to finish them off when an energy bolt shot from out of nowhere and blasted him to the ground.

The Rangers stared in amazement as a mysterious robot-figure stepped out of the shadows.

"Who is it?" gasped Yellow Ranger.

"Or what is it?" asked Pink Ranger.

Red Ranger noticed a familiar symbol on the robot's helmet. "Hey, that symbol ... it's just like Gosei's!" But nobody was listening.

"Stand down, mutants!" commanded the robot. "I am Robo Knight, protector of the environment, guardian of the Earth!"

"Argghh! My slime will take care of you!"
hissed Hisser, shooting a stream of gloop at
the newcomer.

But Robo Knight neatly sidestepped the evil goo and fired a volley
of lasers from his Robo Blaster. As they hit Hisser with deadly accuracy,
the slimy fiend dived underground, ready to attack again. Robo Knight
transformed his Blaster into a Robo Blade and thrust it into the ground,
forcing Hisser to resurface.

Hisser flew into the air and
Robo Knight attacked again.

The Rangers watched in awe as Robo Knight slashed at the monster,
showing no mercy. Then, as one, the teenagers leaped to their feet and
shook the slime from their bodies.

"With him fighting on our side, nothing can stop us!" roared Red
Ranger, lifting his fist into the air. "Go, Go, Megaforce!"

Then the re-energized team rejoined the battle and fought harder than
they had ever fought before. Red Ranger did a backflip and charged at
Bigs. Then, when the moment was right, he and the rest of the team used
their Power Cards to summon their Sky Brother Zords and attached them
to their Blasters.

Calling out "Sky Blast!", the five Rangers took
aim and blasted Bigs and Bluefur clean off their feet.

"We need to return to our lair and recharge our powers by bathing in
toxic ooze," laughed Bigs. "But the next time we meet ..."

Bluefur finished his sentence, "... be prepared to die, humans!" Then he
lifted his staff and blasted Robo Knight before disappearing in a shimmer
of ghastly light.

Robo Knight quickly recovered, only to be sent spinning by Hisser.
The robot crashed into a building and disappeared beneath the rubble.

"That's the end of you, metal-man!" gloated Hisser.

But he was wrong. Within seconds Robo Knight emerged from the dust.

"Negative," Robo Knight said, responding to Hisser. Then he inserted a card into his Robo Blaster, calling for his Vulcan Cannon.

"Knight Dynamic, activate," instructed Robo Knight. "Applying maximum force!" Then he fired, and Hisser was wiped out by a fiery blast.

The Power Rangers rushed to Robo Knight's side.

"He used a Power Card," gasped Red Ranger.

"Just like ours," Yellow Ranger added.

"You stopped that monster cold," Pink Ranger said to Robo Knight.

"Or not," roared a voice. Hisser was back and somehow he had grown to a giant size. He stomped furiously towards the Rangers.

"I'm not just bigger," he boasted. "I'm badder." Then he transformed himself into a Giant Hisser Vehicle and blasted the Rangers with all his might.

"Stand back," commanded Robo Knight, pulling out his Morpher. The Rangers watched as he inserted a card and changed into the Lion Zord. He flew straight at the Giant Hisser Vehicle and rammed it with all his might. Then, much to the Rangers' amazement, he flew to a tractor and hooked onto it to create the Lion Mechazord.

The Giant Hisser Vehicle slammed into Lion Mechazord and trapped him behind a stone wall. But luckily, Lion Mechazord could not be beaten so easily. He smashed through the wall and rolled towards his enemy.

"Rocks cannot stop me," boomed Robo Knight as Lion Mechazord. "I was buried underground for centuries. I will complete my mission."

"Keep coming!" sneered the Giant Hisser Vehicle, as he unleashed a fiery blast. "You're about to be scorched and torched!"

Then he used his tail to whack an enormous boulder at Lion Mechazord, who activated some wheel missiles and rolled on.

"You have threatened Earth ... all threats must be eliminated," Robo Knight, as Lion Mechazord, roared. Then, as he unleashed a barrage of wheel missiles, he proclaimed, "Knight Power Charge!"

The missiles hit their target – the Giant Hisser Vehicle – accurately. "Objective completed," Lion Mechazord said. The battle was won!

The Rangers rushed over as Lion Mechazord morphed back into Robo Knight.

"How come Gosei never told us about you?" asked Emma.

"We want to know all about you," said Troy.

Troy held his hand out in friendship. But without a word, Robo Knight turned his back and walked away.

Meanwhile, deep beneath the Earth's crust, Bigs and Bluefur watched the scene from their cavernous lair. Vrak was there too.

"Poor Hisser," muttered Bigs. "I thought he had what it takes to flatten those Rangers."

"Hisser might have succeeded if that Robo Knight hadn't appeared," snarled Vrak.

"I say the first thing we have to do is recycle that robotic tin can," declared Bluefur.

As Vrak headed out of the cave, he said, "I have a plan. I must find out how to make him work ... for me!"

Faraway, on a distant island, the Rangers gathered before Gosei at their Command Centre.

"How come you didn't tell us there was a sixth Ranger?" asked Gia.

"I didn't tell you because he had been dormant until today," explained Gosei patiently. "Much like your Zords, Robo Knight comes from the Earth. He was created aeons ago with the sole mission to protect this planet. He has the qualities of a true knight – sharp reflexes, the fearlessness of a lion and an unwavering commitment to protecting nature."

"So, he is on our side," said Troy.

"Yes," replied Gosei. "But after such a long hibernation it appears he has lost some of his memory. Robo Knight's computer brain clearly doesn't recall that I created him and that you are his allies."

"Can you fix him?" asked Noah.

Gosei hesitated. "Robo Knight is a highly complex, artificially intelligent machine. He needs to relearn that his mission and yours are the same. Teaching him that will be tricky, but it is up to you to win him over as an ally ... that is your challenge!"